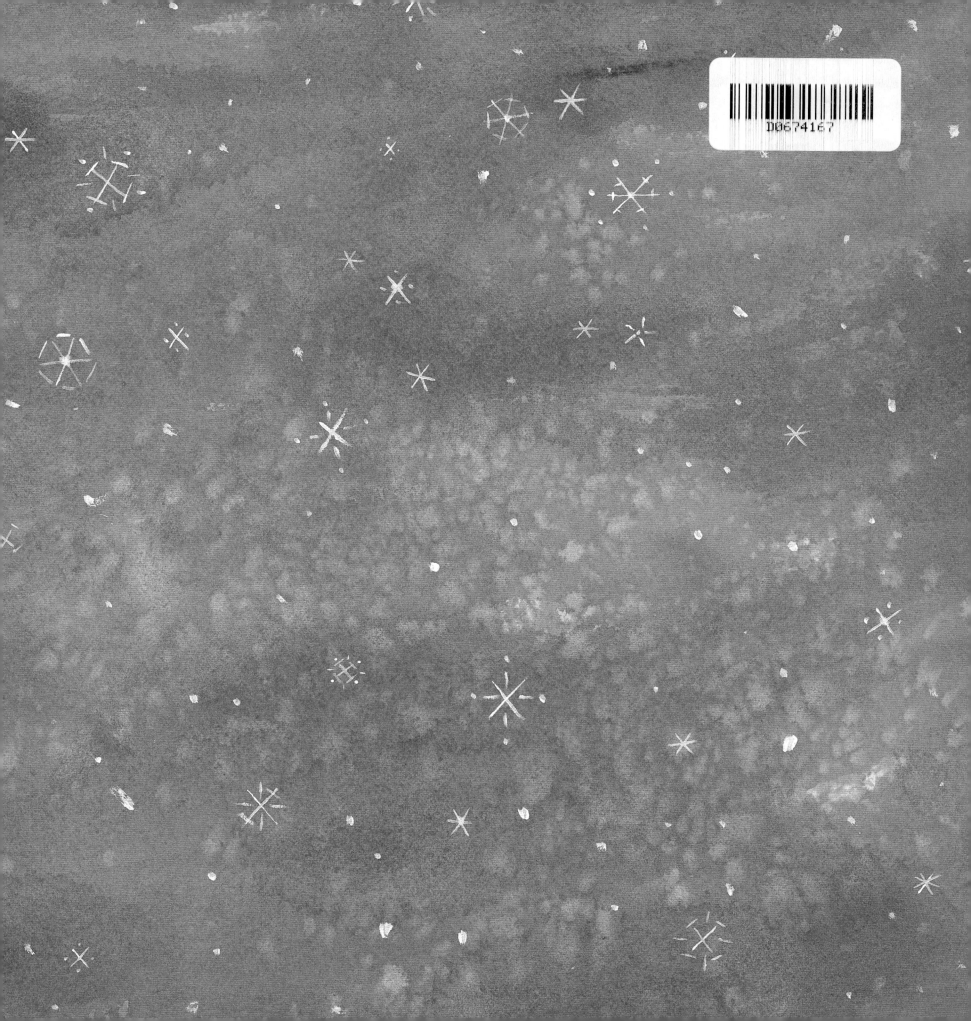

For Janet ~ G L   For Noah ~ T W

LITTLE TIGER PRESS
An imprint of Magi Publications
1 The Coda Centre, 189 Munster Road, London SW6 6AW
www.littletigerpress.com

First published in Great Britain 2006
This edition published 2007

ISBN 978-1-84506-379-5

A CIP catalogue record for this book is available from the British Library

Printed in China
2 4 6 8 10 9 7 5 3 1

Little Honey Bear
and the Smiley Moon

Gillian Lobel

Tim Warnes

LITTLE TIGER PRESS

London

Little Honey Bear couldn't sleep.
Through his bedroom window the
moon was shining, as bright as day.
The snowy woods glimmered in
the brilliant moonlight. And surely
the moon was smiling at him!

"Why, hello Moon!" cried Little
Bear. And he rushed out into
the glittering woods.

There in the moonlight was Lily Long Ears, making snow hares.

"Hello, Little Honey Bear," said Lily. "Couldn't you sleep either?"

"Oh Lily," said Little Bear, "the moon sailed right in front of my window, and she *smiled* at me!"

"Me too!" said Lily. "She's so big and smiley tonight, I just had to come out to say hello."

She showered Little Bear with snow. "Catch me if you can!" she cried, and darted away through the trees.

They ran through the moonlit woods into a wide snowy meadow. High above hung the moon and right across the frozen meadow ran a shining silver pathway.

"It's a pathway to the moon!" cried Little Bear. "Just think, Lily — we could walk all the way to the moon and say hello."

"Little Honey Bear," squeaked a tiny voice. "Can I come too?"

"'Course you can, Teeny Tiny Mouse," said Little Bear.

So off along the moonpath went the three friends.

"What shall we do when we get to the moon?" asked Lily.

"We shall have tea," said Little Bear. "We shall have mooncakes and moonjuice!"

"What are mooncakes like, Little Honey Bear?" asked Tiny Mouse.

"Why, they're round, and flat
and silvery," said Little Bear.
"And very sweet, of course."
"Let's go then!" squeaked
Tiny Mouse.

Suddenly the night grew colder.
A crisp wind whipped the snow
into little flurries. The path to the
moon grew steeper and steeper.

"It's an awful long way to
the moon," gasped Tiny Mouse.
"My little paws are freezing."

So Little Bear scooped Tiny
Mouse into his paw, and set him
on his big shoulder.

"That's much better!" said
Tiny Mouse, tucking his toes
into Little Bear's thick furry coat.
"My paws are happy now."

Up and up ran the moonpath towards
the very top of the hill. Snowflakes stung
their eyes and whirled into their ears.

"Do you think we'll get there soon, Little Honey Bear?"
gasped Lily. "Only my ears are getting rather cold!"
As she spoke a great cloud blew in front of the moon . . .

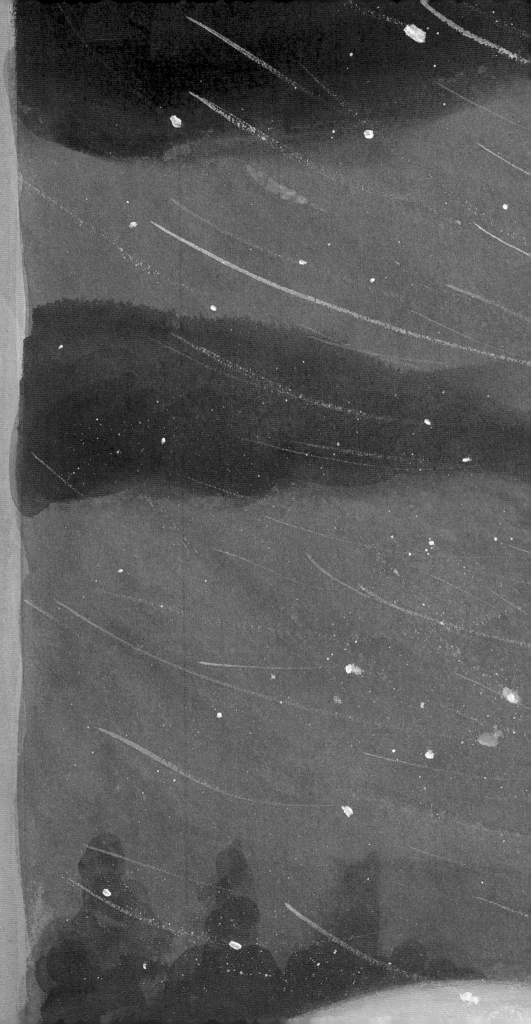

. . . and the moonpath disappeared. Suddenly it was very dark.

"I don't like it, Little Honey Bear," said Lily. "I don't like it at all!"

"I d–d–don't think I want to go to the moon after all," said Tiny Mouse. "Even for mooncakes."

So off they set down the hill.

Down and down they slipped and slithered, until they reached the woods.

"Perhaps the moon is cross and doesn't want to see us after all," said Little Honey Bear.

"I want to go home," quavered Tiny Mouse.

"Me too!" gasped Lily.

But everything looked
different in the dark,
and they couldn't find
their way home.

The trees creaked and groaned, and the wood was full of shadows.

"I think we're lost," sniffed Little Bear. "And I want my mummy!"

Suddenly a silvery light
flooded the woods. And
up above, bobbing between
the trees, the smiling moon
appeared.

"Hooray!" cried everyone.
And then the moonlight
fell upon a big furry bear,
her arms open wide as she
ran towards them.

"Oh Little Honey Bear,
I'm so glad I've found you!"
cried Mummy Bear. And
she gave them all a very
big bear hug.

"Oh Mummy," said Little Bear. "We were going to have tea with the moon, but then she got cross with us, and hid."

"And we didn't get to drink moonjuice," sighed Tiny Mouse.

"Or taste mooncakes," said Lily sadly.

Mother Bear smiled as she took them all back to the warm bear house for a special moon supper, with golden honey cakes and warm milk to drink.

"The moon wasn't cross. She was there all along," she said, "only the clouds were hiding her!"

"Mummy," said Little Bear later,
as she tucked him up in his bed,
"I did so very much want to go
and see the moon."
  "Why, Little Bear, we
don't need to go to the moon
to see her – she's all around us!"

Little Honey Bear looked through
the window. Every tree was hung
with a thousand glassy rainbows
in the bright moonlight. And then
the moon sailed through the trees
and smiled at him.

"Goodnight, Moon," said Little
Bear, rubbing his eyes. Then he
turned over and fell fast asleep.

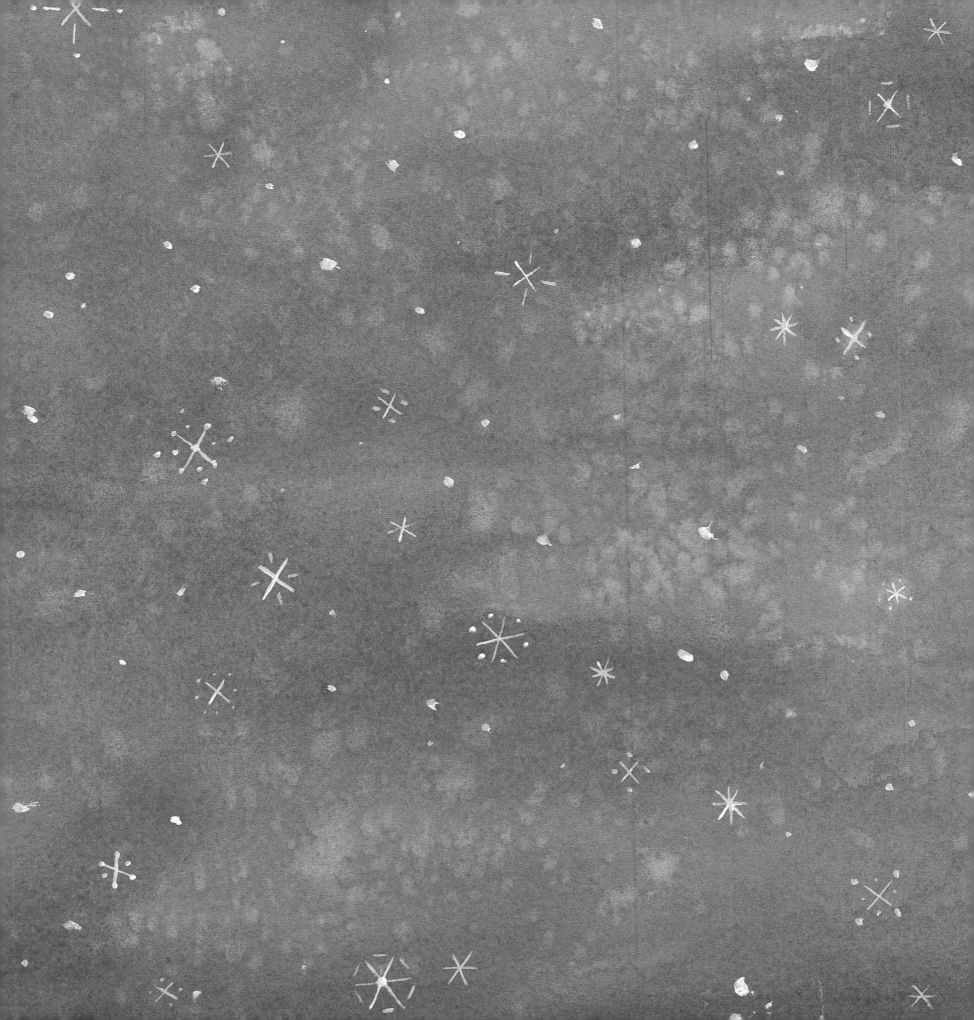